R. Teery

Maynard's Dreams

Maynard's Dreams

David S. Rose

Atheneum 1993 New York

Maxwell Macmillan Canada TORONTO

Maxwell Macmillan International NEW YORK OXFORD SINGAPORE SYDNEY

Atheneum
Macmillan Publishing Company
866 Third Avenue
New York, NY 10022

Maxwell Macmillan Canada, Inc.
1200 Eglinton Avenue East
Suite 200
Don Mills, Ontario M3C 3N1

Macmillan Publishing Company is part of the
Maxwell Communication Group of Companies.

First edition
Printed in Singapore
10 9 8 7 6 5 4 3 2 1
The text of this book is set in 16 point Geometric 706 Medium.
The illustrations are rendered in acrylic on Strathmore paper.

Library of Congress Cataloging-in-Publication Data

Rose, David S., 1947–
    Maynard's dreams / by David Rose. —1st ed.
        p.   cm.
    Summary: Although while he is awake Maynard the cat enjoys such
typical feline activities as chasing birds and squirrels, when he is
dreaming he finds himself in predicaments less pleasant for him.
    ISBN 0–689–31847–2
    [1. Cats—Fiction. 2. Dreams—Fiction.] I. Title.
PZ7.R7148May 1993
[E]—dc20   92–43146

to Marilee

Like many cats, Maynard spends a lot of time hunting birds, chasing mice, and, in general, being a little pest. To Maynard these are just ways to pass the time between naps. Maynard loves to sleep anytime, anyplace that looks comfortable enough. One time he even fell asleep on the branch of a tree after chasing some squirrels.

Of course, the birds, the mice, and the squirrels don't see the fun in Maynard's pastimes at all. Even the humans in Maynard's life sometimes tire of the little nuisance. Perhaps a peek at some of Maynard's naptime dreams would help. In some, poor Maynard finds things turned around in unexpected ways.

Snow, Snow, Snow

In one dream, it started to snow. As the snow came down harder, white shapes around Maynard grew larger and larger. Then the shapes slowly began to move right toward him. Maynard walked as fast as he could walk in the snow. The closer the shapes came, the faster Maynard moved. The faster he moved, the deeper the snow got until he couldn't run at all. The white shapes had almost caught up with him when he woke up!

Trapped

For most of his life Maynard had pondered how to get to the birdcage in the family room. In one dream a ladder had been left under the cage. So, naturally, curiosity made Maynard climb up and jump into the cage. Suddenly the door shut behind him. Maynard was trapped. The caught cat had plenty of time to wonder who had set the ladder under the birdcage!

Ice-Cold

Maynard dreamed he was outdoors. He was so cold he felt like a Popsicle and wondered what flavor he would like to be. He had never been this cold before. Then, with one leg in midair, he froze in his tracks. He could not take another step. For hours he just waited, wondering what to do, hoping no dogs would happen by. Later the sun came out and grew so hot that the snow and everything cold, including Maynard, started to melt . . . and never stopped.

The Wishing Well

Maynard dreamed that he and some friends were walking one day, looking for some trouble to get into. They came to a path that they hadn't noticed before and decided to find out where it led. At the end of the path was a wishing well. After careful thought, all four cats wished they lived in cat paradise. But to their horror, they were instantly turned into mailboxes and birdhouses. Though they were surrounded by birds on a quiet country road, mailboxes and birdhouses weren't quite how they had pictured paradise.

Top of the World

One afternoon Maynard dreamed he was sitting on a platform. The platform was higher than a fence post, higher than the porch roof, higher than he had ever been before. He was almost as high as the clouds. Maynard could see for miles and miles. Then he heard a strange noise. Maynard peeked over the edge of the platform. Right beneath him, just out of reach, were three woodpeckers busily pecking away at the pole holding him up.

The Swim

Maynard was on a log that had fallen over a stream. He was patiently waiting for some tasty fish when he lost his balance and fell into the water! But the shock quickly passed as he found himself having fun swishing his tail and slipping through the water. Maynard was surprised to notice that he had no interest at all in the fish swimming with him. It was when he had odd cravings for worms and turned to look at his tail that horror set in!

Center Ring

Maynard dreamed he was in a circus parade. He was in a cage being pulled through the streets of a city with people cheering him along the way. The parade led to a large tent. When he entered, there were cheers, from the audience this time. Maynard raised his head proudly as the show began. Maynard was the star performer. He was the wild jungle cat . . . but then he saw mice dressed as clowns. Were they there to tame him, or had he been tamed already?

Ticktock

In a most peculiar dream, Maynard was the face of an old grandfather clock. Every night when the clock struck twelve, the mice would come out and play. From midnight to six in the morning, they would climb and dally back and forth in front of him. Imagine a group of delicious mice within Maynard's reach—and all he could do was mark the time.

The Sky Is Falling

After years of chasing squirrels, the squirrels in one dream finally got revenge. Squirrels from all around gathered in the trees that lined the lane Maynard traveled every day. This dream was different. Acorns were a foot deep by the time the bombardment was done. This day the squirrels reigned.

Low Flying

Maynard dreamed that it was Halloween and that he was on his favorite fence post staring at the moon. Suddenly he was snatched away by a low-flying witch! He found himself soaring through the night sky clinging to the witch's broom. This must be a real witch, Maynard thought with delight. But as they passed the moon, Maynard lost his grip and was flung into the open air. Then Maynard woke up. There wasn't even any candy.

The Chase

After years of happily chasing mice, Maynard dreamed he was being chased around his own house by a giant mouse. Maynard scrambled from room to room with the mouse close behind. When Maynard could run no more, the mouse picked him up by the tail, and Maynard was left hanging upside down. How embarrassing! It was certainly one proud mouse. Maynard dreaded what game the mouse had planned next.

The Present

Santa had just placed him there and vanished. Imagine a cat being left as a Christmas present, with a bright red bow around his neck, hanging in a stocking from a fireplace mantel! Maynard heard bells coming from the chimney as Santa's sleigh rushed off. Now all he could see was a Christmas tree and a room filled with decorations. That night seemed to last forever. When morning came, Maynard heard the pitter-patter of children rushing toward the room. That's when Maynard woke up.

. . . and guess where he was? In the arms
of one of his favorite humans! What a relief!
   Sometimes, after dreaming, Maynard decides
to stop chasing birds and mice and squirrels and
to be less of a pest. But only sometimes. . . .